# A Note from Michelle about My Two Best Friends

Hi! I'm Michelle Tanner. I'm eight years old. Do you know what's one of the worst things in the world? It's when you have two best friends who want you to choose between them.

It's not fair! I really like Cassie Wilkins—she and I have been best friends forever. But I also really like Mandy Metz—she's the new girl in school, and we have so much in common. She lives in a really big house, just like me!

Luckily, my big house is full of people who give great advice. There's my dad and my two older sisters, D. J. and Stephanie. But that's not all.

My mom died when I was little. So my uncle Jesse moved in to help Dad take care of us. So did Joey Gladstone. He's my dad's friend from college. It's almost like having three dads. But that's still not all!

First Uncle Jesse got married to Becky Donaldson. Then they had twin boys, Nicky and Alex. The twins are three years old now. And they're so cute.

That's nine people. Our dog, Comet, makes ten. Sure, it gets kind of crazy sometimes. But I wouldn't change it for anything. It's so much fun to live in a full house!

**FULL HOUSE™ MICHELLE novels**

The Great Pet Project
The Super-Duper Sleepover Party
My Two Best Friends
Lucky, Lucky Day
The Ghost in My Closet
Ballet Surprise
Major League Trouble
My Fourth-Grade Mess

Available from MINSTREL Books

# FULL HOUSE™
# Michelle

## My Two Best Friends

### Cathy East Dubowski

A Parachute Press Book

A MINSTREL® BOOK

PUBLISHED BY POCKET BOOKS

New York   London   Toronto   Sydney   Tokyo   Singapore

A MINSTREL PAPERBACK *Original*

 A Minstrel Book published by
POCKET BOOKS, a division of Simon & Schuster Inc.
1230 Avenue of the Americas, New York, NY 10020

A Parachute Press Book
Copyright © 1995 by Warner Bros. Television

FULL HOUSE, characters, names and all related indicia
are trademarks of Warner Bros. Television © 1995.

ISBN: 0-671-52271-X

First Minstrel Books printing July 1995

10  9  8  7

A MINSTREL BOOK and colophon are registered trademarks of
Simon & Schuster Inc.

Cover photo copyright © 1994 Dualstar Entertainment Group, Inc.

Printed in the U.S.A.

# My Two Best Friends

# Chapter

# 1

♥ "You're squushing me!" eight-year-old Michelle Tanner squealed. She squirmed in between her two big sisters. The three of them were packed into the backseat of the family car with all their school gear.

"Michelle, could you move your book bag?" asked seventeen-year-old D.J. "My foot's asleep!"

"Hey—watch out for my science project!" screeched Stephanie, who was twelve.

"First stop—Fraser Street Elementary," their father, Danny Tanner, sang out from the driver's seat.

Danny's friend Joey Gladstone hopped out of the front seat. He held Stephanie's science project while Michelle crawled over her to get out.

"Scoot, little one," Joey said, "or I'm going to be late for my audition!" Joey was a stand-up comic. He had moved in to help out when Michelle's mother died. That was when Michelle was a baby. So Joey was like part of the family.

Michelle yanked her backpack out of the car. Then she gave Joey a quick kiss. "Good luck!" she said.

She waved as Joey jumped back into the car and the "Tanner Taxi" took off.

*Briiiing!* The school bell rang. Michelle hurried toward her classroom.

She loved school. At school she could be special. At home she felt lost in a crowd. Michelle loved her family. But it was so big.

"Michelle—you remembered!" Michelle's best friend, Cassie Wilkins, cried. Cassie was waiting by the classroom door.

Michelle grinned. "How could I forget?"

Both girls had on hot-pink sweatshirts with ballerina teddy bears. That's what they'd given each other for Christmas.

Their pink leggings matched, and so did their baby-blue high-top sneakers.

Michelle wore her long strawberryblond hair in a ponytail. With a pink scrunchie. So did Cassie.

"Cassie, you have such good taste!" Michelle said.

"Ditto!" said Cassie.

3

Arm in arm, they hurried into Mrs. Wexley's third-grade classroom.

Their cubbies were side by side. They hung up their backpacks—both were blue. They even sat next to each other.

Just like every year since kindergarten. That's how long they had been best friends.

"Look!" Michelle said. She flipped open her pink notebook and pulled out a sheet of paper. "I wrote out some messages in our secret code. I made you a copy too."

"Cool!" said Cassie. "I love the colored markers!"

"But don't let *anybody* else see it," Michelle said. "It's top secret! We're the only two people in the universe who know this code."

Cassie nodded and crossed her fingers

**4**

over her heart. That was their secret sign for promises.

The very first message said:

ECRET ODE:

ROP HE IRST ETTER N ACH ORD!

"It looks like a foreign language written down," Michelle said. "Like French. Or German. Or maybe Martian!"

But Michelle knew Cassie could read it in a minute. It said:

SECRET CODE:

DROP THE FIRST LETTER IN EACH WORD!

*Briiiing!* The last bell rang. All the kids scrambled to their seats.

Mrs. Wexley was writing spelling words on the board.

"Good morning, class," she called out.

Michelle liked Mrs. Wexley. She was always smiling. And she always smelled good too—like perfume and chalk. She never yelled at her students. But somehow everyone knew this was a class where you did not make trouble!

Mrs. Wexley began to check attendance.

Just then there was a knock at the door. "Excuse me, Mrs. Wexley," said the principal, Mrs. Homewood. "May I see you for a moment, please?"

Mrs. Wexley stepped out into the hall. She pulled the door almost all the way closed. Michelle could hear their voices. But she couldn't make out what they were saying.

Michelle turned back to her notebook. She practiced writing her name in cursive.

A moment later Cassie tapped her on the shoulder. "Hey, who's that?" she whispered.

Mrs. Wexley led a girl to the front of the room. Michelle had never seen her before.

The girl was tall and pretty with long, curly dark hair. She stared at the class with big brown eyes. She clutched her pink notebook as if it might jump out of her arms. Michelle guessed she was nervous.

Some of the kids started whispering. The girl's eyes flicked downward toward her shoes.

"I've got a surprise for you this morning," Mrs. Wexley announced. "We have a new student in our class. Please say hello to Amanda Metz. She likes to be called Mandy."

Some of the kids said hello.

"Mandy just moved here from New Jersey," said Mrs. Wexley. "We're so glad to have her. And I'm sure all of you will help her feel right at home."

Mandy Metz smiled a little. But Michelle could tell she was still nervous.

"Now . . ." Mrs. Wexley's eyes swept the room. All the seats were taken except one—right next to Michelle. "Here you go, Mandy." She led Mandy to the seat. "You can sit right here."

Mandy sat down. She glanced at Michelle with a shy smile.

"Mandy, this is Michelle Tanner," said Mrs. Wexley. "Michelle, will you please be Mandy's study buddy?"

Michelle sank down in her seat a little bit. Beside her, she heard Cassie groan. Michelle had never been a study buddy before. But she knew what it meant.

She had to stick by Mandy's side for

her first week. She had to show her around, sit with her at lunch, and trade phone numbers in case Mandy needed help with homework.

Michelle glanced over at Cassie. She was used to doing *everything* with her best friend. What would it feel like to spend the whole week with the new girl?

# Chapter 2

 Michelle couldn't say no to Mrs. Wexley.

"Okay," Michelle replied at last.

"Thank you, Michelle," Mrs. Wexley said with a big smile.

Mandy Metz turned to Michelle and said, "Hi."

"Hi," Michelle answered.

She couldn't think of anything else to say.

"Oh, look," said Mandy. "We have the same notebook." She held up hers.

It was the same color and style as Michelle's.

"Hmm," said Michelle. Then she felt Cassie poke her in the ribs. "Oh! This is my friend, Cassie Wilkins."

Mandy and Cassie exchanged hellos.

"All right, class," Mrs. Wexley said. "Take out your math workbooks, please, and turn to page twenty-seven."

Michelle pulled out her book and whispered to Cassie, "Don't worry. I'll still save you a seat at lunch."

Michelle felt like Mandy's tour guide that morning. First she showed her where everything was in the classroom. Mandy liked their pet mice, Boris and Natasha.

At snack time Mrs. Wexley asked Michelle to take Mandy around the school. So Michelle showed her where the office was. How to find the library. And most important—where all the bathrooms were!

In art class they found out they had the same favorite colors: pink and blue.

On the playground they found out they both liked the swings better than the jungle gym.

At reading time they found out they both liked mysteries.

Finally it was lunchtime.

"Children who are buying lunch line up first," Mrs. Wexley called out.

About half the class got in line—including Cassie. Cassie's mom *always* made her buy lunch in the cafeteria. She said a hot lunch was more nutritious.

"Not if you can't eat it!" Michelle and Cassie always joked.

"Okay," said Mrs. Wexley. "Lunchbox and lunch-bag people next."

Michelle and Mandy grabbed their lunches from their cubbies. Then they stood in line.

"Hey, I can't believe it!" Mandy held up her lunch. "You and I have the same lunchbox! And I bought mine back in New Jersey."

"That *is* weird," Michelle agreed. "I never knew people in New Jersey had the same lunchboxes!"

Then Michelle noticed Cassie at the front of the line. She stared at Michelle with a strange frown.

*What's wrong with her?* Michelle wondered.

Soon they marched down the hall toward the smell of food.

The cafeteria was noisy, as always. Michelle led Mandy to her favorite table. It was by the window, so they could look out at the playground. She saved a seat for Cassie too.

"Sorry," Michelle told Mandy. "It always smells like fried bologna in here."

Mandy opened her lunchbox and laughed. "My old cafeteria smelled like fried bologna too!"

*At least Mandy is easy to talk to,* Michelle thought.

"Do you like your new house?" Michelle asked her.

"I really do," Mandy answered. "There's just one problem."

"What?"

"Too many people!" Mandy said. "My family is huge!"

"I bet it's not as big as mine," Michelle bragged. "There's *nine* at my house. And a dog!"

"Hey! I have nine at my house too!" said Mandy. "My mom just got remarried. My stepfather has three kids. So with my two older sisters that makes eight. And my grandmother makes nine. We have a dog too."

**15**

"I have two older sisters too," said Michelle.

"Awww, too bad!" Mandy said. She and Michelle laughed.

Michelle told Mandy all about her family.

The Tanner house was pretty big. But it was stuffed with people from top to bottom.

Her uncle Jesse and his wife, Becky, lived in the attic. They had twin boys named Alex and Nicky. They were three years old—and into everything!

Michelle, her dad, and her two sisters filled up the middle of the house.

Dad's best friend, Joey, lived in an apartment in the basement.

Nine people plus Comet, their dog. That made a very full house!

"You know, Michelle," Mandy said shyly, "I didn't want to move and leave all my friends behind. I thought the people here would be really different. But you're so nice. And we're actually a lot alike."

Michelle smiled and started to speak—SMACK!

Michelle jumped. She looked over at Cassie's spot. Cassie had just plopped her lunch tray down on the table. A little fruit cup had sloshed over the mystery meat. A couple of green peas rolled across the table and onto the floor.

Above the steaming vegetables, Cassie's face was steaming too.

# Chapter

# 3

♥ Michelle stared at her best friend. *What's wrong?* she asked with her eyes.

Cassie just looked away. She ate her lunch without saying a word.

Michelle guessed Cassie didn't want to talk about it in front of Mandy.

Mandy didn't seem to notice. She chattered away as if they were all the best of friends.

"How can you eat that mystery meat?" she teased Cassie. "It looks like gray Play-Doh."

Michelle laughed. Cassie just cut off a bigger bite and stuffed it in her mouth.

"Anybody want half of my granola bar?" Mandy asked.

"I'll take it," said Michelle. She reached for it, then stopped. "Oh—do you want it, Cassie?"

Cassie made a face at Michelle. "You *know* I hate granola bars!"

"Oh, yeah," Michelle said. "I forgot."

"Want to hear a joke?" Mandy asked. "My new brother told it to me."

"Sure," said Michelle.

"What's a mermaid's favorite lunch?"

"I don't know," said Michelle. "What?"

"Peanut butter and *jellyfish* sandwiches!"

"Hey, that's what *I* brought today!" Michelle joked.

She and Mandy could hardly stop giggling. Then Michelle saw that Cassie wasn't laughing at all.

Michelle stared at her best friend. Cassie loved jokes. So why did she seem so unhappy? "What is it?" Michelle asked her. "What's wrong?"

Cassie just shook her head. "Nothing," she said. But her face said *something—something big*.

Mandy wiped her mouth with a napkin. Then she cleaned up her place and closed her lunchbox. "Michelle," she said quietly, "I have to go to the bathroom. Could you help me find the closest one?"

"Um, sure," said Michelle. "See you later, Cassie?"

Cassie just shrugged and attacked her fruit cup.

Michelle hurried after Mandy to throw out her trash. She glanced back at Cassie. She looked so sad sitting all by herself, Michelle thought. Maybe she should go back and sit with her till she was finished. . . .

"Ready, Michelle?" Mandy asked.

Michelle felt torn in two directions. But she was Michelle's study buddy. It was her job to help Mandy out.

*Cassie will understand*, Michelle told herself.

*I hope. . . .*

Being a study buddy kept Michelle very busy. She hardly had time to talk to Cassie all week.

But being a study buddy wasn't all that bad. Each day she liked Mandy a little more. Each day they discovered new things they had in common.

On Tuesday they went to chorus. Miss Pennyfeather had tryouts for special parts in the next school concert. She made a big fuss over Mandy's singing.

She picked Michelle and Mandy to sing a duet.

On Wednesday Mandy was kickball captain and picked Michelle for her team. Michelle told Mandy to pick Cassie next. But Kiana Gregory picked Cassie for the other team. Kiana's team almost won too, but Mandy scored the winning point in the last thirty seconds!

On Thursday the class went on a field trip to the Science Museum. Mrs. Wexley assigned everyone a partner. She asked Michelle and Mandy to be line leaders. Line leaders got the front seat on the bus.

Cassie got stuck being Sidney Wainwright's partner. Sidney was a big know-it-all and always had a runny nose. He usually sat with Matthew Bronski. But Matthew was out sick.

Cassie and Sidney wound up sitting together all the way in the back of the bus. Cassie did not look happy.

By the end of the day Michelle could tell she and Mandy were starting to be real friends.

But Michelle was worried about her friendship with Cassie. She didn't feel like they were best friends all week.

So Michelle almost cheered when it started to rain.

On rainy days Michelle and Cassie always rode the bus home—and sat together. Michelle couldn't wait to hang out with her best friend.

But that afternoon Cassie hurried out the door. Michelle looked for her when she got to the bus.

Cassie was sitting with Arnold McKenzie.

*Huh?!* Michelle thought. *She hates Arnold!*

24

Michelle waited a second for Cassie to glance up. But Cassie just ignored her. Michelle walked down the aisle past Cassie and sat down by herself.

Arnold got off at the first stop. Michelle started to move up. But Cassie quickly put her backpack in the empty seat. Then she turned her face to the window.

Michelle dug a sheet of notebook paper out of her pack. She wrote a quick note in their secret code.

EAR ASSIE,

LEASE ON'T E AD T E. E'RE TILL EST RIENDS.

OVE,

ICHELLE

Michelle folded the note in half. Then she tossed it up to Cassie's seat.

Cassie glared at it a moment as if it were a bug she'd like to squash. Then she picked it up. She didn't read it. But she did tuck it into the front pocket of her pack.

Michelle went home and did her homework. She kept hoping Cassie would read her note and call.

But she didn't call all afternoon. She didn't call during dinner.

But during dessert the phone rang!

Stephanie, D.J., and Michelle jumped up at the same time. "It's for me!"

"No, me!"

"It's *mine!*"

Danny held up his hand for silence. "Who knows?" he pointed out. "It might even be for me."

He picked up the phone. "Hello, Tanner residence," he said.

"Is it Cassie?" Michelle whispered.

Danny shook his head and kept talking. "Oh, hi. Really? That's wonderful.... I've heard a lot about Mandy too. Uh-huh.... That sounds nice. Let me ask her."

Danny held the phone to his chest. "It's Mrs. Metz—Mandy's mother. She wants to know if you'd like to spend the night at their house tomorrow night, then go to that new indoor amusement park the next day."

"The Gold Rush!" Michelle cried. She'd been dying to go there! She jumped up and down and nodded yes!

"That sounds great, Mrs. Metz. Thanks," Danny said into the phone. Then he turned to Michelle. "Here, Mandy wants to talk to you."

Michelle took the phone. "Hello?"

"Hi, Michelle!" Mandy said. "I'm so glad you can come."

"Me too," Michelle answered. "I've been dying to go to the Gold Rush."

"There's just one thing I have to ask you," Mandy said. "Do you like roller coasters?"

"I love them!" said Michelle.

"Me too!" squealed Mandy. "My sisters won't ride them. They're afraid they'll throw up!"

Both girls giggled.

"Oh, Michelle," said Mandy. "We're going to have a great time!"

"I can't wait!" said Michelle. "See you tomorrow!" She hung up and danced around the room. "All right!"

"Hey, Michelle," her dad said. "Mrs. Metz says Mandy really loves her new school. And she thinks it's all thanks to you."

That made Michelle feel pretty good.

"You know, honey, I'm really proud of you," Danny said. "Sometimes people are not always nice to the new kid in school. Or even worse, they ignore them. You're really doing something special by being a good friend to Mandy."

"Well," said Michelle, "Mrs. Wexley kind of made me do it at first. But Mandy's really nice. So it turned out to be easy."

Michelle went upstairs to the room she shared with Stephanie. She had two more multiplication problems to work on. She plopped onto her bed and opened her notebook.

But it was hard to keep her mind on her math problems. She kept thinking about how much fun she and Mandy were going to have.

The phone rang again. A few seconds later Danny called upstairs, "Michelle! It's for you!"

Michelle raced down the stairs and

picked up the phone. Maybe Mandy wanted to talk about the Gold Rush some more. "Hello?"

"Hi, Michelle."

It wasn't Mandy. It was Cassie!

"Thanks for your nice note," Cassie said. "I . . . I'm really sorry about how I acted today."

"That's okay," Michelle said. "I'm just glad you're not mad at me anymore."

"Best friends forever?" Cassie said.

"Best friends forever!" Michelle said.

They both crossed their fingers over their hearts.

"Guess what?" Cassie exclaimed. "Mom says I can invite you over to spend the night on Friday."

"Great! We can—" Michelle stopped. "Did you say Friday night—as in *tomorrow* night?"

"Of course," said Cassie. "Mom said

she'd pick us up at school. She'll even take us to the mall to rent a video if we want to."

Michelle didn't know what to say. Somehow she didn't want to tell Cassie she was spending the night at Mandy's house. She had a funny feeling it would make Cassie mad.

"Michelle? Are you still there?"

Michelle blurted out the first thing that came to her mind. "I have to help Dad bake a cake Friday night. And I, uh, promised Becky I'd help D.J. baby-sit the twins all day Saturday."

"Oh," said Cassie. She sounded disappointed. "What kind of cake?"

"Um, a birthday cake!" said Michelle quickly. "For D.J."

"For D.J.?" said Cassie. "I thought her birthday was in December, like my mom's."

"Did I say D.J.?" Michelle said. "I

meant to say—Uncle Jesse. That's right. And it's not his birthday. It's—it's his anniversary! With Aunt Becky! It has to be really special. We're going to make this great big guitar . . ."

Cassie didn't say anything for a moment. Then she said, "Maybe we can do it next Friday."

"Sure, sure!" Michelle said, almost out of breath. "Well, uh, it's getting late. I've got to go brush my teeth! See you tomorrow!" She slammed down the receiver.

Michelle stared at the phone. She couldn't believe what she had just said! She glanced around. Had anyone heard her?

No. No one was nearby.

Michelle sank down on the bottom step of the stairs. She propped her head in her hands. What had she done?

The Tanners' golden retriever trotted

over. He gazed at Michelle with his friendly dark eyes.

"Oh, Comet. I just did something really dumb," she confessed. "I just told my best friend a big fat fib!"

Comet licked her cheek. He almost seemed to understand.

"I just did it so I wouldn't hurt her feelings," Michelle explained. "It's what Dad calls a white lie. So that makes it okay . . . sort of. Doesn't it?"

Comet barked and trotted off.

Michelle gulped. It *was* the nice thing to do. Wasn't it?

Then how come her stomach felt so weird—like she'd eaten twelve pieces of pizza?

# Chapter 4

💗 "Michelle! Wait up!" It was Friday morning. Mandy waved from the kiss-and-go car lane in front of the school. "I've got something to tell you about to-night!" she called out.

Mandy ran up to Michelle. She stopped to catch her breath. She flipped a black curl away from her face.

"What's up?" Michelle asked.

"Guess what?" Mandy exclaimed. "My stepdad got this neat tent for his birthday.

He said we could sleep in it tonight if we want. Mom said it's okay."

Michelle gulped. "You mean outside? In the dark?"

"No!" Mandy laughed. "Even better. We'll set the tent up in the living room. That way we won't have to sleep with my sisters. They both snore!"

Michelle giggled. "That sounds like fun!"

"Cool!" Mandy grinned. "Be sure to bring your sleeping bag, okay?"

"Okay!" Michelle said.

A tingle went down her spine. She felt eyes burning into her back. She turned around and froze. Cassie was walking up right behind her. Was she spying on them? How much did she hear?

"Hi, Cassie," Michelle said.

"Hi," Cassie said bluntly.

All three headed into the classroom. Mandy stopped by Mrs. Wexley's desk to ask a question. Cassie followed Michelle to her desk.

"Michelle!" Cassie whispered suspiciously. "What was all that about tonight?"

"Tonight?" Michelle asked. What could she say? "Uh, nothing. Just something Mandy said I should watch on TV."

Cassie started to ask what. But Mrs. Wexley instructed the class to take out paper for their spelling test.

Michelle slumped into her seat. *I told my best friend another lie!* she thought. *And it wasn't even a little white one. This one was a great big purple whopper!*

Things could not get any worse, Michelle thought.

And then they did.

That afternoon Mrs. Wexley announced a new project. "We're going to do projects about American pioneers," she said. "I'd like you to work in pairs. Each pair should do a presentation on anyone in American history who was a pioneer. I have a list of suggestions if you need ideas. Projects will be due a week from Monday."

Mrs. Wexley went around the room, counting off partners. Then she got to Michelle, Cassie, and Mandy. She realized she had one student left over.

"Michelle, Mandy, and Cassie," Mrs. Wexley said. "How about if you three work together as a group?"

Michelle peeked at Mandy. She was smiling and nodding.

Michelle peeked at Cassie. She was not smiling or nodding.

Michelle sort of smiled. "Of course . . . I guess."

Mrs. Wexley told the class they could work on the projects for the rest of the afternoon.

Michelle led Cassie and Mandy to an

art table in the corner of the room. "I was thinking—"

"I've got an idea," Cassie interrupted.

Michelle looked sideways at Cassie. Cassie never interrupted.

"We can make a covered wagon somehow," Cassie said in a rush. "Then we can do a skit. Something about pioneers in the Old West. It'll be great!"

She smiled at Mandy. "I've read *all* the *Little House on the Prairie* books. So I know all about covered wagons and stuff."

Michelle nodded. "That sounds good." She turned to Mandy. "What about you?"

"Well . . ." Mandy bit her lip.

"Go ahead," Michelle insisted. "Tell us what you think."

"Okay," she said. "Don't you think a lot of kids are going to do pioneers from the Old West?"

Cassie frowned. "So?"

"So it's kind of . . ." Mandy's face turned pink. "Cassie, I don't mean to hurt your feelings. But, well, it's kind of boring."

"Boring!" cried Cassie.

*Uh-oh,* Michelle thought. "You know, guys, maybe we could—"

"So my idea is boring, huh?" said Cassie. "Do *you* have a *better* idea?"

Mandy thought real hard for a moment.

"I know!" she cried. "Let's do something *really* different. Most people think of the past when they think about explorers. But what about the future? Let's do space explorers! We can call it 'Pioneers in Space'!"

"Hey!" said Michelle with a smile. "That sounds pretty—"

"I don't want to do something 'different,'" snapped Cassie. "I want to do covered wagons!"

Mandy looked surprised. "You don't like my idea? Come on, Cassie. Think about it. 'Pioneers in Space' could be really cool."

Cassie grabbed Michelle's hand. "Tell me, Michelle. You want to do covered wagons too. . . . Don't you?"

Mandy looked a little embarrassed— but determined too. She gently grasped Michelle's other hand. "I guess it's up to you to break the tie, Michelle. But just think how *different* space explorers would be. Come on—it'll be fun."

Both girls stared at Michelle—and waited for her to say something. Michelle felt like the rope in a tug-of-war! She didn't know what to say.

"Tell her," Cassie insisted. "You want to do *my* project. Right?"

"Well . . ." Michelle said in a tiny voice. "I'm not exactly sure."

"But, Michelle!" cried Cassie. "We're best friends! We always do the same thing!"

*Briiiing!*

"Okay, class!" Mrs. Wexley called out. "Work on your projects over the weekend. I'll give you more time on Monday."

The noisy class bustled around her. Kids grabbed backpacks and rushed toward school buses. But Michelle was in no hurry. She slowly pulled her books from her cubby. She stuffed them into her backpack one by one.

But it didn't matter how slowly she went. She couldn't escape. Cassie and Mandy both waited for her by the classroom door. They both looked determined to win her vote!

*Great*, thought Michelle. *Now what do I do?*

*Honk! Honk!*

Michelle peeked out at the curb. She

could see Mr. Tanner waiting inside the car.

"Dad!" Michelle cried. " 'Bye, Cassie. 'Bye, Mandy," she said quickly. Then she slipped past them and dashed for the car.

"I took off from work early," Danny said as Michelle hopped into the car. "So I thought I'd swing by and get you." He nodded toward Cassie and Mandy. "Want to offer your friends a ride home too?"

"No, thanks!" Michelle cried. She slammed the door and locked it. "They want to walk!"

Michelle slunk down in her seat. Her dad pulled the car away from the curb. She saw Cassie and Mandy grow smaller in the rearview mirror.

*What am I going to do?* she wondered. *How can I keep two friends happy at the same time?*

# Chapter 5

❤ *"EEEK!* Captain Tanner!" cried Mandy. "What's that?"

Michelle shone her space flashlight into the dark night. "Battle stations, Major Metz!" Michelle shouted. "Alien beings are about to attack! I will send our robot guard dog to protect us!"

Michelle peeked out of a small tent at Mandy's living room. She and Mandy had switched off most of the lamps. Mandy's silver-haired terrier barked at the shadows they created with their flashlights.

"This tent makes such a cool space-ship!" Michelle said with a giggle.

"Just think how much fun our project could be if we did something like this," Mandy said. "What do you think, Michelle? Wouldn't this be way more fun than covered wagons?"

"You're right," Michelle admitted. It *was* fun. But how could she make Cassie see that?

"Maybe we should write some of this down," Mandy said thoughtfully. "We could use it for our project. Cassie might really like doing space explorers if she sees some of our ideas."

"Maybe," said Michelle. But she didn't really think so. She crawled out of the tent to get her notebook. She flipped it open to some clean notebook paper.

A single sheet of paper with colored writing fluttered out.

She bent down to grab it. But it sailed into the tent—right under Mandy's nose.

*Uh-oh!* thought Michelle, crawling back into the tent.

"Hey!" Mandy giggled. "Want to make paper airplanes?" She picked up the paper. "Or paper spaceships! We could use them to send secret messages!"

She started to fold the piece of paper. Then she saw that it was covered with colored letters. "Hey, cool! What's this?"

"Oh, nothing really . . ." said Michelle. She reached out to grab the sheet of paper.

Mandy pulled it away. "Is it a secret code?" she asked. "I *love* secret codes. Oh, let me see if I can figure it out!"

"But—"

"I've got it!" Mandy cried. "It says 'SECRET CODE: Drop the first letter of every word!' "

*Now I'm really in trouble,* thought Michelle. *If Cassie ever finds out . . .*

Suddenly they heard a strange high-pitched voice outside the tent. "Greetings, Earthlings!"

Michelle and Mandy shrieked!

Legs appeared in the doorway. "Welcome to our planet. I come bearing gifts of food."

A head peeked in. "Anybody want some popcorn?"

"Mom!" Mandy said with a laugh.

"Thanks!" said Michelle. She liked Mrs. Metz. She reminded her a little of Aunt Becky.

"I'm going up to my room to read," Mrs. Metz said. "You girls let me know if you need anything else. But let's not stay up too late. We've got a lot of rides to tackle tomorrow!"

Michelle and Mandy ate loads of popcorn. They talked about their project some more. Then they turned out the lights and told ghost stories—but not too-scary ones!

"You know, Michelle," Mandy said, "I'm really glad Mrs. Wexley picked you to be my study buddy."

"Me too," Michelle said. She was really starting to like Mandy a lot. They were having so much fun together.

Michelle sort of forgot about how her secret code was not so secret anymore.

# Chapter 6

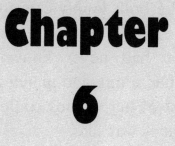 "Hey, Michelle!" cried Mandy. "Let's ride the Rocket Junior one more time!"

"All right!" Michelle shouted. That was their absolute favorite!

Michelle and Mandy were having a great time at the Gold Rush amusement park. They liked all the same rides. They even bought the same souvenir—pink and blue cowgirl hats. The words GOLD RUSH were printed across the front in gold glitter.

Michelle thought Mandy's family was great too. It was a lot like hers. *Big!* They had to take both family cars to fit every-body in!

Michelle had never known anybody else who had a mix-and-match family like hers. Most of her friends couldn't under-stand what it was like.

Even Cassie didn't really understand. She was an only child. Her house was al-ways nice and neat and quiet. Sort of like a museum.

But Mandy knew exactly what it was like to live in a house full of people. Sometimes it was wonderful. Sometimes it was awful! But there was always *something* going on. Sort of like an amuse-ment park!

Mandy got permission from her mom to ride the Rocket Junior again. Michelle and Mandy hurried over to wait in the long line. They told knock-knock jokes to keep from getting bored.

"Knock-knock," said Mandy.

"Who's there?" said Michelle.

"Orange."

"Orange who?"

"Orange you glad we're friends!"

"Yes!" said Michelle, giggling. *You know,* she thought, *it's neat to have two best friends.*

Suddenly someone tapped her on the shoulder—hard!

*"Michelle!"*

Uh-oh. Michelle stopped laughing. *It can't be,* she thought. *It's not!*

Slowly she turned around.

*It is!*

"What are you doing here?" Cassie demanded with an angry scowl.

"H-hi, Cassie," Michelle muttered. "How are you?"

Michelle felt as if she had just gotten caught robbing a bank. Cassie thought she was home baby-sitting the twins!

Michelle wished she hadn't lied to Cassie. And she really wished she and Mandy weren't wearing those silly matching hats!

How in the world could she explain everything to Cassie? Tell another white lie? Tell the truth?

But she didn't get a chance to say a thing. Just then an empty roller-coaster car glided up in front of them.

"Next!" the attendant growled. He herded the three girls into the car—first Mandy, then Michelle, then Cassie. Kind of a "best friend" sandwich—with Michelle in the middle!

*Clang!* The man locked the safety bar in place. The roller coaster started to climb a hill . . . very, very slowly.

"Ou aid ou ere aby-itting," said Cassie.

Michelle gulped. She crossed her fingers. She crossed her toes. She crossed her eyes. *Please, please, please* . . . she wished toward Mandy. *Don't let Cassie know you know. . . .*

"Aby-itting?" Mandy asked—in their secret code. "Hen?"

Cassie gasped. She turned to Michelle with angry tears in her eyes. "Oh, Michelle!" she whispered. "Not our secret code!"

Michelle's face turned scarlet. She started to explain. She wanted to tell Cassie it was all an accident. It didn't mean anything anyway. Not really.

But the roller coaster plunged down its first hill. Her words were whipped from her mouth.

Michelle had a sinking feeling in the pit of her stomach. But it had nothing to do with the ride.

She had a feeling that as soon as they could all catch their breath—Cassie was never going to speak to her again!

# Chapter

# 7

♥  Michelle would never forget that moment when Mandy used Michelle and Cassie's secret code. The look on Cassie's face!

Michelle wanted to explain. But when the ride stopped, Cassie jumped out and disappeared into the crowd.

Michelle called her Saturday night—and all day Sunday. But her mom kept saying that Cassie was "busy." Cassie wouldn't even come to the phone!

Monday morning Stephanie yanked Michelle's covers off. "Hey, Sleeping Beauty—rise and shine!"

Michelle grumbled and pulled the covers over her head.

"Oops! Sorry—*Grumpy!*" Stephanie teased. She grabbed a sweatshirt and leggings and dashed for the shower.

*I can't get up,* Michelle thought. *I can't go to school—ever again! I can't face Cassie!*

"Michelle!" Danny called up the stairs. "Are you up?"

Michelle pulled a pillow over her head. She tried to go back to sleep.

A few minutes later Stephanie was back from the shower. "Hey, Michelle—what's the matter? You sick or something?"

*That's it!* Michelle thought. *I'm sick! I can't go to school if I'm sick!*

"Yeah . . ." Michelle croaked. She tried to sound weak.

"Really?" Stephanie sat down on the bed. "What's wrong?"

"I feel terrible," Michelle groaned.

Stephanie jumped up. "I'll go get Dad!"

She nearly slammed into Uncle Jesse and Alex right outside the door. Jesse was giving Alex a horseback ride down to breakfast. He stuck his head in the door. He and Alex looked like a two-headed monster. "Hey, what's wrong?"

"I think Michelle is sick," Stephanie said, squeezing past Uncle Jesse.

"Who's sick?" Aunt Becky asked from the hallway.

"Who's sick?" Nicky repeated as he wiggled down from Aunt Becky's arms.

"Dad!" Stephanie yelled down the stairs. "Come here—quick!"

Soon everyone in the house crowded into Michelle and Stephanie's room. Everyone spoke at once.

That was one of the problems with a full house. No matter what happened, everybody had to get into the act!

Michelle pulled the covers over her head.

But at last D.J. calmed everyone down. "Let me talk to her alone," D.J. said, shuffling everyone out.

Danny didn't look too sure. "Well, okay. But I'll go get the thermometer."

D.J. plopped down on the edge of the bed. "Okay, kiddo. What's *really* going on?"

Michelle slipped the covers down a little. Just her eyes peeked out. "Huh?"

"Come on," D.J. said. "I know a faker when I see one."

"Really?" Michelle sat up. She brushed the hair out of her eyes. "How?"

D.J. laughed. "Because I've tried it enough myself!"

Michelle sighed. She was caught! "Okay," she admitted. "I'm not really sick. I just don't want to go to school."

Then Michelle told D.J. all about her

"two best friends" problem. She even explained about the lies she'd told Cassie.

"That happened to me one time," D.J. said. "But in the end it all worked out."

"What happened?" Michelle asked.

"One of the girls moved away," D.J. said with a smile.

"Thanks a lot," Michelle said.

"Listen," D.J. said, "you've got to talk to Cassie. Apologize for telling her things that weren't true."

Michelle groaned. "She'll never forgive me."

"Oh, Michelle," D.J. said. "You and Cassie have been friends a long time, right?"

Michelle nodded.

"It would take a lot to break up your friendship. She's probably just a little jealous of your new friend. That's all. In fact, I bet she's over it by now."

"You really think so?"

D.J. nodded. "I'm sure of it. These kinds of things—they're never as bad as you think."

D.J. gave Michelle a big hug. Maybe D.J. was right, Michelle hoped. Michelle got dressed and went to school.

And D.J. was right. It wasn't as bad as she thought. It was worse!

Cassie wouldn't talk to Michelle. She wouldn't even look at her. At their desks she scooted away as far as she could.

And at lunch she sat with Arnold McKenzie again!

Michelle felt rotten. And she was worried too. How could they do their project together if they weren't even speaking?

Even more important: What if she lost Cassie's friendship forever?

That afternoon Michelle sat between Cassie and Mandy.

"Listen, guys," she began. "We've got to

start working on our project. We don't have much time left. Let's decide what we want to do."

"Still want to be my best friend?" Cassie whispered.

Michelle nodded.

"Then prove it!" Cassie whispered. "Say you want to do *my* idea."

Michelle sighed. At least Cassie was talking to her! But she felt pretty guilty about the whole thing. She'd never meant to hurt Cassie. And she didn't want to lose her friendship. Maybe she could still fix things!

"I think we should do Cassie's idea," said Michelle. "The covered-wagon thing."

"But, Michelle!" Mandy said, surprised. "That's not fair. You said you liked *my* idea better!"

"When did you say that?" asked Cassie.

"When she spent the night at my house," Mandy cut in.

"You spent the night at her house too?" asked Cassie.

Before Michelle could answer, Cassie jumped up and dashed back to her desk.

"Wait, Cassie!" Michelle cried. "Come back. We'll do your project. I promise!"

Mandy's chair screeched on the floor as she got up. "What about me and what I think?" she asked. She looked mad too, as she stalked off to her desk.

Michelle put her head down on the table. Now she'd done it. She had hurt Cassie's feelings and Mandy's too. She'd made them both mad.

*Cassie and Mandy have something in common now,* Michelle thought. *They both hate me!*

"Last week I had two best friends," Michelle mumbled into her arms. "Now I don't have even one!"

# Chapter

# 8

♥ That night Michelle felt really sad. So sad she couldn't swallow any of her dessert.

"Hey, what's the matter, pumpkin?" Danny asked. "Something wrong with my chocolate raspberry surprise?"

Michelle shook her head.

"I'm having trouble with friends," she said. "I'm trying to stay friends with Cassie. But I like being friends with Mandy too."

"Remember that old camp song?" her

dad asked. He cleared his throat, then sang: " 'Make new friends, but keep the old. One is silver, and the other gold.' "

Stephanie and D.J. snickered.

Nicky and Alex bounced in their chairs and tried to sing along.

"Ah, yes, my favorite camp song," said Joey.

Jesse sang along too. It was obvious he didn't know the words. He just made them up, but he sounded good. He was actually the lead singer in a band.

It was kind of funny, but Michelle didn't even smile.

"Hey, cheer up, kiddo," Joey said. "Listen. I'll give you some of my latest jokes. Try them out on Cassie and Mandy. They'll crack up. Then they'll forget all about being mad."

"*Your* jokes?" teased Danny. "Come on. We don't want to make them *cry!*"

"I think you should write them each a note," Stephanie suggested. "If that doesn't work, bribe them with gifts!"

"Oh, brother!" said D.J.

Now everyone at the table had something to say.

But Michelle didn't cheer up. Funny stories and advice were one thing. But real life with real people was another.

Aunt Becky got up to help Danny clear the table. "It'll work out, honey." She gave Michelle a little hug. "A couple of months from now, you'll forget all about this."

"Maybe," said Michelle. *A couple of months could take forever!* she thought.

Later that evening Michelle heard squeals upstairs. She poked her head into the bathroom. Uncle Jesse was giving the twins a bath. They had smeared soap bubbles all over their cheeks and chins.

"Look at our beards!" Alex called out.

"We're shaving!" Nicky said proudly.

"Aren't they cute?" Jesse said. He was crazy about his kids. "Michelle! I've *got* to get this on video. Can you watch Nicky and Alex for two minutes? I'll get my camcorder!"

"Sure," said Michelle. She knelt down on the fluffy bathmat. She folded her arms on the side of the tub. The twins were always fun to watch. Maybe it would cheer her up.

"Look at me!" said Alex. He piled a mound of soap bubbles on top of his head.

Michelle grinned. "Cute!"

"No!" shouted Nicky. "Look at *me!*" He scooped up some bubbles and blew. Chunks of foam flew into Michelle's hair.

"Hey," Michelle said. "Watch out—"

"Michelle!" Alex squealed. "Look!"

He grabbed the soap and bombed his rubber ducky with it. *Splash!*

"Waahh!" Nicky cried. "He got soap in my eyes!"

Michelle squeezed out a wet washcloth. "Come here, Nicky." She held Nicky's chin and gently wiped the soap from his eyes. "Are you okay now?"

Nicky grinned and splashed his brother. "Michelle likes me best."

"Uh-uh," said Alex. He splashed back harder. "She likes me best! Michelle— look at me!"

Waves of water sloshed over the side of the tub.

"Hey, stop it, guys!" Michelle shouted. "You'll flood the whole house!"

Michelle grabbed some towels and mopped up the water.

Nicky and Alex grew quiet.

"Are you mad, Michelle?" Nicky said.

Michelle had to laugh. They both looked like drowned rats! "No, I'm not mad," she said. She tried to dry their hair with a towel.

"Listen," she told them. "I don't like either one of you best."

The three-year-olds looked puzzled. "You don't like us?" Alex asked softly.

Michelle rolled her eyes. "Of course I do!" she said. "What I mean is—I like you both. I love you both. It's not a contest."

She kissed each boy on the top of his soggy head. "Alex—you've got all my Alex love. And, Nicky—you've got all my Nicky love. There's enough to go around for everybody."

The twins smiled happily. They soaped each other up again.

"Perfect!" Jesse cried from the door-way. He held the camcorder up to his eye and started shooting. "Thanks, Michelle."

A few hours later Michelle turned over in bed. She squinted at her glow-in-the-dark clock. It was way past her bedtime. Stephanie had already turned off her reading lamp and fallen asleep.

But Michelle couldn't sleep. She couldn't stop thinking about her friends. *You mean ex-friends,* she reminded herself.

Just then her dad peeked in.

By the glow of the night-light she could see him tiptoe into the room. He stopped at Michelle's chest of drawers to re-arrange some stuffed toys.

She watched him straighten Stephanie's covers so they were nice and neat. Then he kissed her good night.

Next he crept over to Michelle's bed.

He fluffed out her coverlet. Then he spotted Michelle peering at him.

"Michelle," he whispered. "Are you still awake?"

"No," Michelle whispered back.

They both giggled. Danny sat down on the edge of her bed.

"Still worried about Cassie and Mandy?" he asked softly.

Michelle nodded. "I like them both, Dad," she whispered. "I really do. I wish I didn't have to choose between them."

"Maybe you don't have to choose," said Danny.

"What do you mean?" Michelle asked. "I thought you could have only one best friend."

"That's not true, honey," said Danny. "Look at me. Joey and I used to be best friends in college. Then Jesse became my new best friend. But I didn't stop being best friends with Joey."

"That's right!" said Michelle. A smile spread across her face. "You mean I could stay best friends with Cassie . . . and still be friends with Mandy too? All *three* of us could be best friends at the same time?"

"Why not?" said Danny.

"Thanks, Dad," said Michelle. She gave him a big hug. Then she lay back on her pillow.

Danny tucked Michelle in. "Just remember, sweetie. *Best* friend doesn't have to mean *only* friend." Then he tiptoed out and closed the door.

Michelle turned over and snuggled down into the covers. She thought about what her dad had said. Then she remembered what she had told the twins. *It's not a contest.*

How could she ever choose between Alex and Nicky? It would be impossible. They were too cute. And they looked exactly alike!

Or between her sisters Stephanie and D.J.? She couldn't! They were *both* annoying!

"Just kidding..." Michelle mumbled through a yawn.

Stephanie sat up in bed with one eye half open. "Huh?"

But Michelle was too sleepy to talk anymore.

*Now,* she thought as she fell asleep, *if only I could think of some way to show Cassie and Mandy ...*

# Chapter

## 9

♥ Michelle bolted out of bed the next morning. She was the first one to scarf down Danny's orange walnut waffles. She was in a huge hurry to get to school.

Michelle had an idea!

At school she wrote two notes. One for Cassie. One for Mandy. Both notes said the same thing:

IG EWS! LEASE EET E T UNCH!

*Big news! Please meet me at lunch!*

Michelle repeated to herself. *They'll figure it out.* Both her friends knew the code now.

At lunchtime Cassie and Mandy *both* tried to sit with Arnold McKenzie.

But Michelle wouldn't let them. She dragged them over to their table by the window. She made them sit down.

Cassie folded her arms and stared off to the left.

Mandy crossed her legs and stared off to the right.

"Listen, guys," Michelle announced. *"I'm* taking over this project."

That got their attention!

"We can't agree on a project idea," Michelle went on. "So we'll just go with mine."

"Yeah, right," muttered Cassie, rolling her eyes.

"Hmmph!" Mandy mumbled.

"Wait a minute," said Michelle. "Give me a chance."

Michelle grinned like a cat with a secret. Then she told them her fantastic idea.

Michelle took a bite of her sandwich . . . and waited.

Cassie and Mandy stared at each other for a moment.

Michelle could tell—neither one wanted to give in first.

"Come on," Michelle said. "You know it's a *great* idea."

Slowly . . . Mandy cracked a smile.

Then . . . Cassie grinned too.

"I love it!" said Cassie.

"Let's do it!" Mandy cried.

Michelle pumped the air with her fist. "Yes!"

Together the three friends began to make plans. . . .

\*      \*      \*

The next Saturday Mandy and Cassie met at Michelle's house. Their projects were due on Monday.

Cassie brought poster board and colored markers.

Mandy brought some props.

Michelle showed them the costumes she'd dug up.

"Cool!" squealed Cassie.

"This is going to be the best!" Mandy agreed.

A few minutes later the door to the kitchen opened. Michelle saw her father peek into the living room.

She winced when she saw him gasp. Paper and scissors and markers lay all over the furniture. All over the floor.

A great big cardboard box stood in the middle of the room. It said SPACEMAKER II REFRIGERATOR. THE LATEST IN ENERGY-SAVING APPLIANCES.

"Michelle!" Danny whispered. "Look at this mess!" He couldn't stand big messes.

Michelle ran over. "But, Dad—look!" She pointed at her friends.

Cassie and Mandy were talking. They were giggling. They were sharing markers. And ideas.

"We're all friends again!" Michelle exclaimed. "Isn't it great?"

"Yes, pumpkin," Danny agreed. "And that's worth a mess any day." Then he bit his thumb. "But you will help me clean it up, won't you?"

Michelle patted him on the arm. "Sure, Dad. For you, anything!"

That afternoon Michelle posted an invitation on the refrigerator:

SNEAK PREVIEW!!!

## Full House: Michelle

A new play by

Michelle Tanner * Mandy Metz * Cassie Wilkins

TONIGHT! 7 PM

ADMISSION: FREE!

At five minutes past seven Michelle, Cassie, and Mandy waited nervously in the living room. They had strung up a curtain made out of two sheets.

Michelle poked her head out.

She tapped her foot as everyone paraded into the living room.

They sat on the couch. The chairs. The floor. Nicky, Alex, and Comet kept switching seats.

"It's a full house!" Michelle whispered to Cassie and Mandy.

At last her audience settled down. Michelle stepped out in front.

"Thanks for coming, everybody!" she

announced. "And now—on with the show!"

Michelle ducked behind the curtain. She pushed the play button on Stephanie's boom box.

Music played as Michelle and Cassie pulled open the curtain. Mandy stood in the middle and held up a sign. Handwritten in colored markers, it said:

LITTLE HOUSE ON PLANET EARTH

The music stopped abruptly.

Michelle turned off the boom box. She hurried to center stage. Now she was holding a microphone. She was wearing a pink skirt and a blue linen blazer.

"That's my microphone," Jesse whispered proudly.

"Hey!" said D.J. "And that's my brand-new jacket!"

"Oops!" said Michelle. "I forgot to ask. May I borrow your new blue jacket ... please?"

D.J. folded her arms and pretended to be mad. "We'll talk about this later, kid!"

Michelle grinned and turned to the audience.

"I'm Michelle Tanner. And this is a special report!" she said. "It's about America's pioneers. Brave people who boldly go where no man—or woman—or *kid*—has ever gone before."

Michelle walked several steps to the right. "This is American astronaut Mandy Metz," she said.

Mandy grinned through a big plastic space helmet. Her white space suit looked almost real—it was just a little baggy.

Danny poked Joey with his elbow. "Isn't that your Halloween costume from last year?" he whispered.

"Uh-huh," Joey whispered back. "I'm glad I kept it."

"Ahem!" Michelle shot them a look.

Danny and Joey put a finger to their lips and nodded.

"Astronaut Metz," Michelle said, "you have explored many new planets, haven't you?"

"Yes," said Mandy. "I was the first person to land on Mars."

"You are a real pioneer," Michelle said. "But I understand you have some exciting news."

"Yes," Mandy said. "On my last trip into space, I made a new discovery. There is a hole in the time barrier! Today I am going to travel back in time!"

"Good luck!" Michelle said.

Mandy walked over to her "spaceship." It was called *Spacemaker II*. It was the size of a cardboard refrigerator box. It was painted bright pink and blue.

Mandy opened a cut-out door and got inside. She waved through a cut-out window.

Michelle stepped back and counted, "Three . . . two . . . one . . . *blast off!*"

*Ka-pow!* Cassie popped a paper bag behind the curtain. She tossed a handful of flour into the air.

Danny choked and stared at the carpet. "What was that?"

"It's supposed to be engine noise and smoke—from our rocket blasting off," Michelle said in a stage whisper.

Danny's mouth hung open. "But—"

"Don't worry, Dad," Michelle added quickly. "I promise I'll clean it up."

The "smoke" cleared as Michelle and Cassie yanked the curtain closed. The three girls giggled as they set up the next scene.

Soon Michelle pulled open the curtain again.

Mandy pushed her way out of the cardboard spaceship.

She stopped in front of a "covered wagon."

"Yay!" cheered the twins.

"Our wagon's in a play!" Alex shouted.

Their shiny red wagon was topped with a sheet. It looked like a covered wagon—sort of.

"Greetings!" Mandy called out.

Cassie poked her head out of the back of the wagon. She wore a long flower-print dress and an old-fashioned bonnet.

She pretended to be startled.

"Oh, my goodness!" she cried. "I've seen buffalo on this prairie. I've seen Indians. But I've never seen anything like this!"

Mandy helped Cassie out of the wagon.

"I am just a pioneer—like you," Mandy said. "But I am from the future. I came to learn more about what life was like in your time."

*Hey,* the real Michelle thought suddenly. *How come things got so quiet all of a sudden?*

She peeked around the darkened living room.

No one was talking. A miracle in the Tanner house! They were all watching the play. They liked it!

At last Mandy the astronaut and Cassie the prairie girl stepped into the spaceship together.

Michelle the reporter announced, "Together the two new friends blasted off into space."

*Ka-pow!* Danny winced as another flour "explosion" filled the room.

"Together they would explore another place, another time. True American pioneers. The end."

Then the living room exploded—with cheers and applause.

Michelle and Cassie and Mandy took a bow.

"That was wonderful," said Aunt Becky. "I especially liked the strong female characters!" she added with a wink.

"Michelle, that was great," said her dad. "Your teacher is going to love it. How did you come up with such an interesting idea?"

"Well," said Michelle. "Cassie had a good idea. And Mandy had a good idea. I just sort of smushed them together."

"Ooh," said Danny. He pretended to shudder. "Sounds kind of messy."

"But it worked," said Michelle. She hooked arms with Cassie and Mandy. "Thanks to my two best friends!"

\* \* \*

That night Michelle, Cassie, and Mandy took over the living room. They gathered all their supplies: TV, remote control, popcorn, soda.

Then they spread out their sleeping bags in front of the TV.

"Hey, want to go rollerblading tomorrow?" Michelle asked her two friends.

"Sure," said Cassie. She squirmed backward into her bag.

"I can't," said Mandy. She dug into the popcorn. "My mom signed me up for soccer. This girl on the team named Lauren promised to help me pick out some cleats tomorrow."

"I tried soccer once," said Michelle. "But I never could score. The goalie kept getting in the way of the ball!"

Mandy and Cassie laughed.

"We don't have to like *all* the same things to be friends, do we?" Mandy asked.

"No way!" said Michelle.

"That would be 'boring'!" Cassie added with a grin.

Michelle grabbed the remote control. "Okay, guys. What'll it be? A comedy?"

"A horror movie!" Cassie said spookily.

"MTV!" cried Mandy.

Michelle grinned and clicked on the TV. "Maybe a little of all three."